The SLEEPLESS NIGHTS of the BOY with NO EYELIDS

AND OTHER TWISTED TALES

written by

MARMALADE ATKINSON

with insignificant input from New York Times best seller, G.P. Taylor

Concept, design and layout by Marmalade Atkinson. Art by Alex Thompson and Marmalade Atkinson

**The Sleepless Nights of the Boy with No Eyelids
and Other Twisted Tales™**

Text copyright © 2025 Marmalade Atkinson
Illustrations copyright © 2025 Markosia Enterprises Ltd
Book and cover design and layout © 2025 Marmalade Atkinson

Published by Markosia Enterprises.
PO BOX 3477, Barnet, Hertfordshire, EN5 9HN.
Harry Markos, Director.

FIRST PRINTING, January 2025.

A CIP record for this book is available at the British Library.

Paperback: ISBN 978-1-917459-42-6

Hardback: ISBN 978-1-917459-44-0

eBook: ISBN 978-1-917459-43-3

www.markosia.com

First Edition

The paper used for this book comes from trees. Trees are very
important. They are natural carbon capture units and provide you
with the oxygen you need to read this book. Look after the trees.

To

Foxton

(who was born with both eyelids).

Contents

1. THE SLEEPLESS NIGHTS OF THE BOY WITH NO EYELIDS 09

2. MOULDING MOIRA 55

3. HERBERT'S EXPLODING SHERBET 73

4. AN ODE TO THE DEARLY DECEASED 115

5. CHILDREN 137

The Sleepless Nights
of the Boy with No Eyelids

WARNING

MAY CONTAIN: NIGHT TERRORS, A CLOWN AND UNDERPANTS

Eyelids are a funny thing;

those trifling little flaps of skin.

Imagine life without a pair;

how you'd have to stare and stare.

There was a child; a lidless boy.

For the sake of rhyme, we'll call him Roy.

He had two legs, he had ten toes.

He had two arms, a mouth, a nose.

He had a bright white set of teeth

(and all you should have, underneath).

But Roy looked like a mannequin.

Now where on earth do I begin?

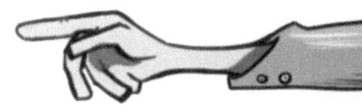

His eyes stuck out like cannonballs;

bulging: you could see them all.

It made him look quite odd and creepy,

weird and wacky; never sleepy.

He couldn't blink. He'd never wink.

His eyes were dry; the whites were pink.

The days were bad; the nights much worse.

Being lidless *was* a curse.

Roy couldn't doze;

he never dreamed.

He lay there and he

screamed

and

screamed.

And while the world was fast asleep,

things close to him began to creep.

Dark shadows

danced across his wall.

The Devil crept in from the hall.

An ancient hag relived her doom

theatrically in fine costume.

This wasn't freaky, not even odd,

but when you're in the

LAND OF NOD

you do not see this ghastly sight

when fast asleep with eyes shut tight.

You do not see this night parade;

the march of those

now long decayed.

You do not see

the dark displays

and morbid moon-lit cabarets.

While other children snoozed in peace,

the Devil tried on poor Roy's fleece.

Then, lit a fire in his grate.

(And all of this by ten-past-eight.)

Roy

sank

FURTHER

down

his

bed;

a surging, soaring sense of dread.

Whilst overhead the chaos grew

and, round and round, a teddy flew.

Just like a lock-in at the pub,

Roy's room became a

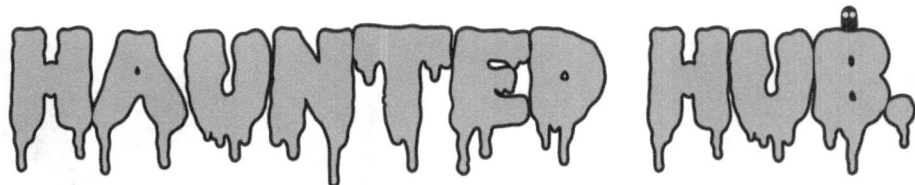

A ghostly party, all the rage.

Ghouls gathered there of every age.

'Why did you have to pick *my* house?'

Roy griped, he grumbled and he groused.

The crone began to toast some ants.
A clown made bunting from his pants.

22

Roy was feeling quite bogged down.

They heard him shrieking in the town

as creatures bungeed from a chair

and others crawled up through his hair.

And then the clown drew out some balls;

he flung them at the doors and walls.

Roy shouted words we can't repeat.

(They

T
U
M
B
L
E
D

out into the street.)

Mum did her best to calm the boy.

These freaks, they had it in for Roy.

She asked the crone to tone it down.

'I'll seize your balls,' she warned the clown.

R
O
A

tried so hard to get to sleep

by counting up some phantom sheep.

Forty winks, a nap, a doze.

Oh! To have some lids to close.

Yet,

every dusk,

the same old thing;

Roy wonders what

the

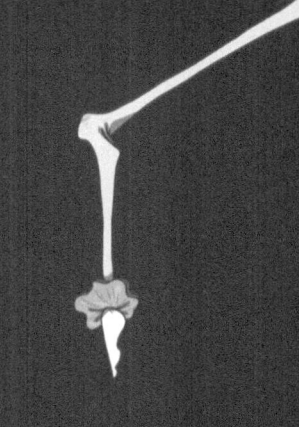

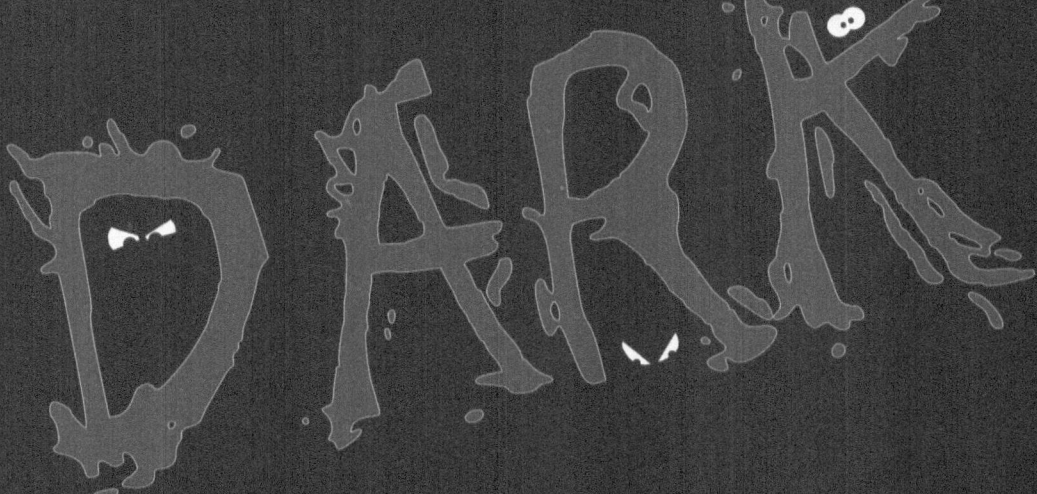

will bring.

His only hope, the mob will bore;

go knock upon another door.

But every time the sun sinks low,

the hag performs her one-hag-show.

The shadows poke his bloated eyes

with twigs and sticks and cold french fries.

And then one night, things got much worse:

the Devil turned up in a hearse.

From out the boot some monsters spilled,

and soon enough Roy's room was filled...

...with creepy critters, bugs and beasts –

a slimy, supernatural feast.

'Order, now!' the Devil shouts

to all the raucous hairy louts.

He then removes a drawstring sack

once resting on his bony back.

Inside, he shoves his scaly hands,

discarding several frying pans.

Sun cream next, prescription shades,

a cocktail shaker, swimming aids.

A pair of shorts embossed with 'HOT'.

A blow-up lilo and a yacht.

He digs, he dives, he delves some more.

He tips the contents to the floor.

A MEGA box of fireworks.

He leers, he sneers, he grins, he smirks.

Like busy bees, they come alive;

tiny sparks shoot from the hive.

They bud, they blossom, then they bloom.

They whizz, they zoom and some go

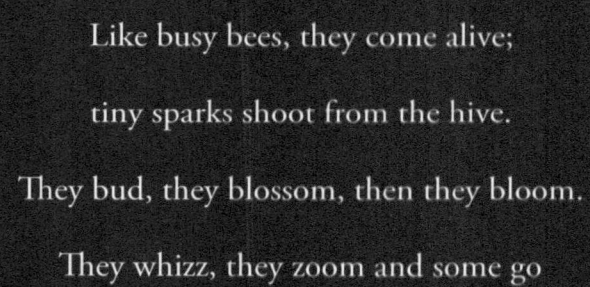

A rage of rockets blast the ceiling.

Wallpaper curls, then starts peeling.

Roy's mother shouts,

'Enough! Enough!'

In her nightie,

she is tough.

She grabs

poor Roy

and then

some thread:

a beigey pink

to match

his head.

Off to work,

on a mission;

time to solve

her son's condition.

An hour later, Roy is back;

above each eye, a curtain track.

But would the curtains do the trick?

Fully lined – they were quite thick.

How wonderful when things go right

for Roy slept soundly all that night.

His guests were snubbed. His guests were bored;

no one likes to be ignored.

Happy now that he could dream, he dreamt of tractors, toys, ice-cream...

...The dreams came thick. The dreams came fast. How glorious to sleep at last!

Refreshed, restored, Roy awoke.

He didn't need his morning Coke.

'Forget the coffee; I'll be right

now I'm sleeping through the night.'

He grabbed his bags, set off for school

in blazer, tie, and blue cagoule.

Then angry winds whipped to a gale

and plucked his curtains

from

their rails.

How Roy cried, his curtains stolen.

Home he ran, eyes red and swollen.

Now what would his mum invent

to end her offspring's sad lament?

First came blinds: Venetian, roller.

Blackout lining with

ANTI-SOLAR ™

It was shutters that she thought up next.

But none of these quite passed the test.

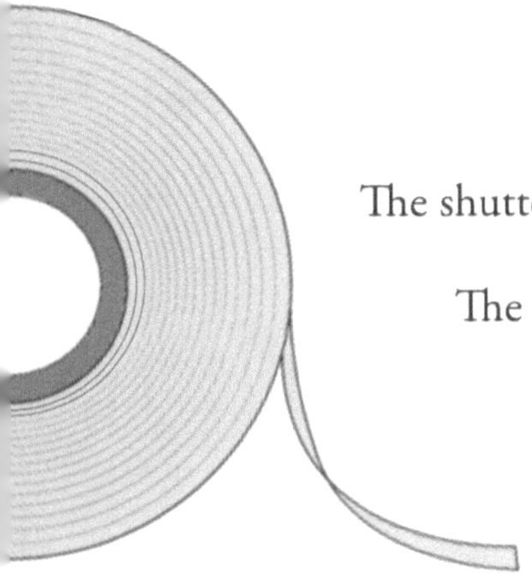

The shutters were clunky, the blinds were a mess.

The lining was itchy, unsightly at best.

Next, she tried buttons and Velcro and glue.

Would Sellotape work? She hadn't a clue.

41

The little old lady at the shop

suggested zips; Mum bought the lot.

She heaved Roy up onto the table

in her attic sewing gable.

She prepped his eyes with *Eye-o-dine,*

then fed him under her machine.

Hovering above: a glinting spike.

The looks of which Roy did not like.

(A VERSE HAS BEEN
REMOVED SO AS NOT TO
UPSET OUR MORE
SENSITIVE READERS.)

and then ...

The whirring stopped; it was done.

It sure as hell had not been fun.

But high above his nose and lips

were now two pairs of sturdy zips.

Roy said goodnight, his face agleam.

He wondered if tonight he'd dream.

He zipped the left eye,

then the right

while mum crept out and dimmed the light.

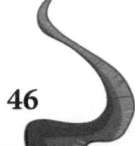

Quickly now, Roy fell asleep

and there he stayed for one whole week.

His mother shrugged, 'It's overtime!

Sleeping in is not a crime.'

But Roy's slumber was not good

despite him getting what he should.

He dreamt the crone was full of lice

and the clown was juggling mice.

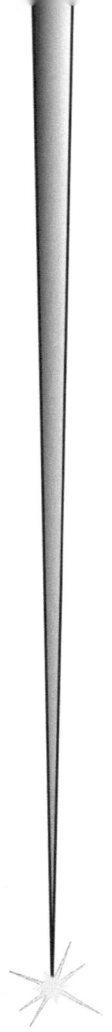

Into a nightmare, Roy had plunged

as, through the darkness, needles lunged.

The Devil cried, the Devil wailed,

and past his bed, on boats he sailed.

Fireworks zipped around his room:

BOOM!
BOOM!
BOOM!
BOOM!
BOOM!
BOOM!
BOOM!

And then the sparks set things alight;

igniting his rug, and Roy with fright.

'Don't worry mate,' the Devil said,

as things poked at him in his bed.

'You're bound to wake up very soon –

it's dull without you in this room.'

But this was not to be the case;

Roy's zips had rusted to his face.

The dream police were after him –

the things they did – well, they were grim.

I trust his mother will realise

that *plastic* zips are best for eyes.

If only Roy had lids built in;

zips aren't needed when you've skin.

It's such a shame to leave Roy there.

Be grateful that his ailment's rare.

And truly hope, if you have kids,

that they are born with both eyelids.

The End

Moulding Moira

Moira

was a good girl,

well-mannered and polite.

But on her thirteenth birthday,

something happened overnight.

A furry mould crept over her:

a musty, fusty coat.

It started at her toes and tips

and finished at her throat.

As she woke, it quickly spread

further up her face;

past her nose, towards her hair

at quite a speedy pace.

Now,

no one wants to wake and find

mildew, blight and rot.

It's bad enough to have erupt

a pimple, zit or spot.

It's certainly *not* what you want

upon your birthday suit.

To find yourself impersonating

old decaying fruit.

As Moira slowly shrivelled up,

cried her mother in distress:

'What's happening to my darling girl?

She's rotting in her dress!'

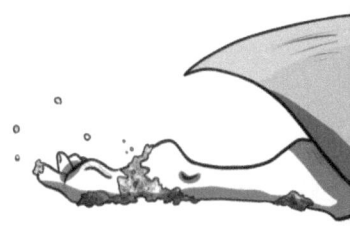

Her brother poked and prodded,

puffs of mould flew everywhere.

A greying kind of candyfloss

replaced her usual hair.

A fetid form of creeping fur

burst from Moira's dress.

Like a werewolf on the turn,

could Moira be possessed?

And with it came a rotten pong

of socks and camembert.

Moira's family didn't want

to breathe polluted air.

They lined their car with newspaper

then shoved her in the back,

cranking up the air-con

until it was full whack.

One speeding ticket later,

the surgery was full.

Slouching here and sprawling there:

children caked in wool.

Was this a new pandemic?

A virus, plague, disease?

Yet none of them were coughing.

No wheezing. Not a sneeze.

The woman at reception

told Moira, 'Take a seat'.

She spritzed the girl in perfume

down to her furry feet.

Moira was eventually called.

She leapt up from her chair.

A fart of dusty, mouldy fluff

escaped into the air.

But all their hopes of remedies,

of cures and wonder-drugs,

were thwarted when the doctor sighed

and gave a sullen shrug.

'We've got no jabs. There are no pills,

no ointment, rub or cream.

It's part of life. It often happens

when they turn thirteen.'

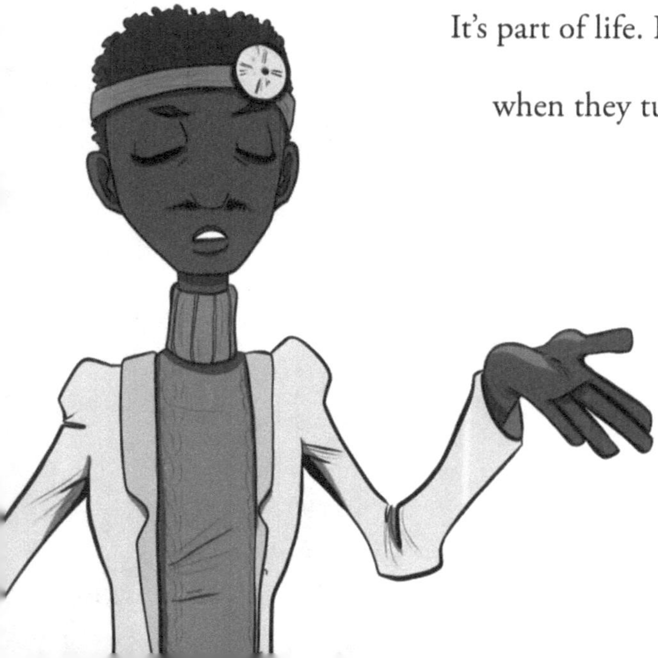

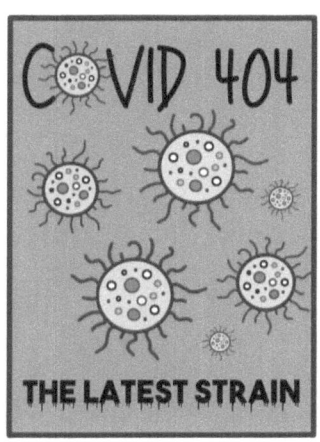
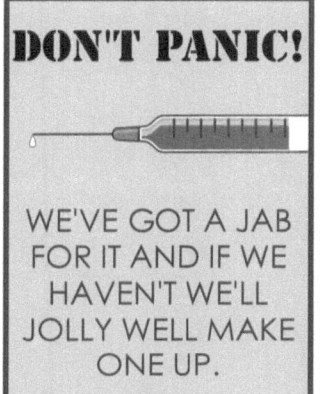

'When she's twenty, if not better,

come and see me then.

(And in the meantime, if she suffers

colds or flu or phlegm.)'

He called for his next patient,

'I'm afraid it's quite a fad.

It seems that when they reach teenage

they nearly *all* turn bad.'

Herbert's Exploding Sherbet

If

be the spice of life,

then Herbert's life was awfully bland...

...for this young boy ate nothing else

than all the sherbet in the land.

He would not eat his porridge.

He would not touch white bread

He wouldn't munch on spicy food,

nor something that was dead.

He'd tried a varied diet –

some of his five-a-day.

But Herbert's tiny taste buds,

in horror, shrank away.

His mother was obliging;

she didn't have much choice.

She'd mix it up with water

to try and make it moist.

She served it up for breakfast.

She served it up for tea.

She served it up in mugs and bowls

and plates upon his knee.

That boy devoured sherbet,

no matter what the brand.

Could it be that Herbert had

a faulty sugar gland?

The neighbours twitched their curtains

and looked on in disgust;

they'd heard that Herbert's lunch box

was full of

FIZZING DUST

The kids at school thought it cool;

their friend did not conform.

Sandwiches, a pack of crisps

and chocolate were the norm.

Herbert was The Sherbet Boy;

his friends thought he was great.

But unbeknown to Herbert,

trouble brewed upon his plate.

One day he turned the TV on;

he sat with Dad and Mum,

resting a bowl of sherbet

on his podgy little tum.

His father dropped his newspaper.

His mother dropped her jaw.

All of them were horrified –

appalled at what they saw.

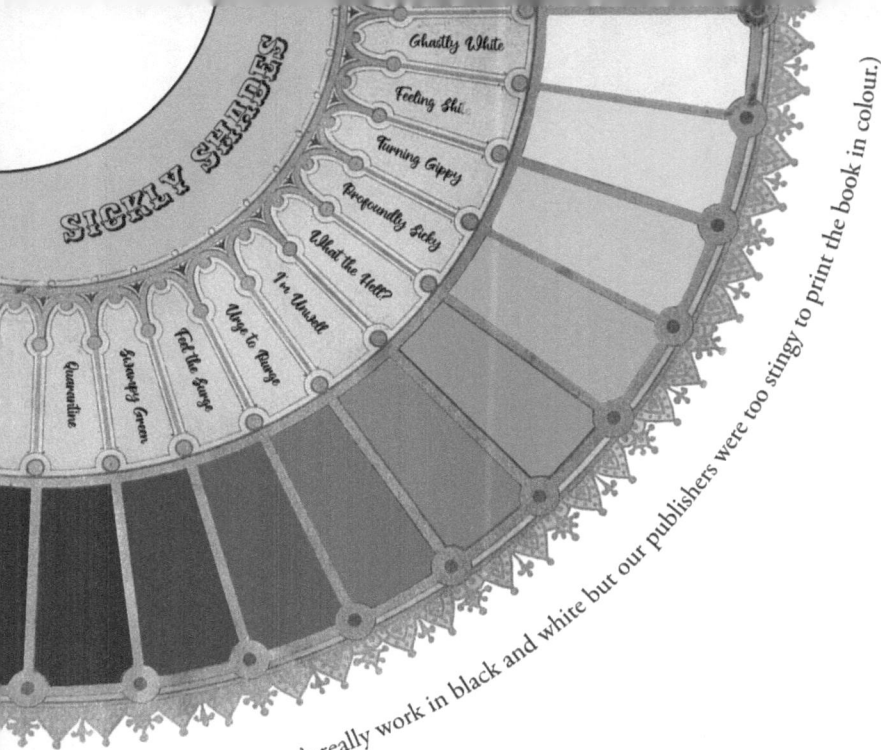

SICKLY SHADES

Ghastly White
Feeling Shit
Turning Gippy
Profoundly Sicky
What the Hell?
I'm Unwell
Urge to Purge
Feel the Surge
Scrungy Green
Quarantine

*(We realise this doesn't really work in black and white but our publishers were too stingy to print the book in colour.)

There was a sherbet shortage.

The country was clean out.

Excess demand in Diddly-Spout

had caused a worldwide drought.

Mum and Dad turned white,

then flushed a swampy green.

And Herbert turned a sickly shade

somewhere in-between.*

Herbert's need for sherbet

was causing lots of grief;

his father had gone bankrupt,

his mum became a thief.

If only they had money,

they could ship it from abroad.

But the import tax, on its own,

was more than they'd afford.

They took a van to Calais,

filled up with duty free.

At Customs there were sniffer dogs;

there was no chance to flee.

A suitcase full of powder

did not go down too well.

First, they got arrested,

then locked up in a cell.

The jail was dark and stinky

but they didn't stay too long.

Sweeteners aren't illegal;

the cops had got it wrong.

Once home, supplies diminished;

sand through an hourglass.

The sherbet hoard they'd got abroad

was disappearing fast.

Nibbles, snacks and munchies

followed breakfast, lunches, teas.

His mum tried him on sugar

and that sticky stuff from bees.

With sherbet off the menu,

what on earth were they to do?

Mum and Dad were at a loss.

Poor Herbert had no clue.

Things were getting desperate,

now supplies were running low.

After much consideration,

Herbert planned a farewell show.

He printed off some tickets

which sold out *really* fast;

news stampedes around a school

when something sounds a blast.

In little time, the day arrived.

Fifty guests confirmed.

Herbert sent his folks for tea

with money he had earned.

As the cab drove them away,

a whistle Herbert blew.

There quickly formed, outside his house,

a long, excited queue.

Every child had brought a chair,

as per the invitation.

The crowd was getting quite immense

and filled with speculation.

Keen not to draw attention,

Herbert swept them through the door,

then swiftly marched them up each step

towards the second floor.

There, he stubbed the tickets

and, with care, arranged the chairs.

If they hadn't paid full price,

they watched from on the stairs.

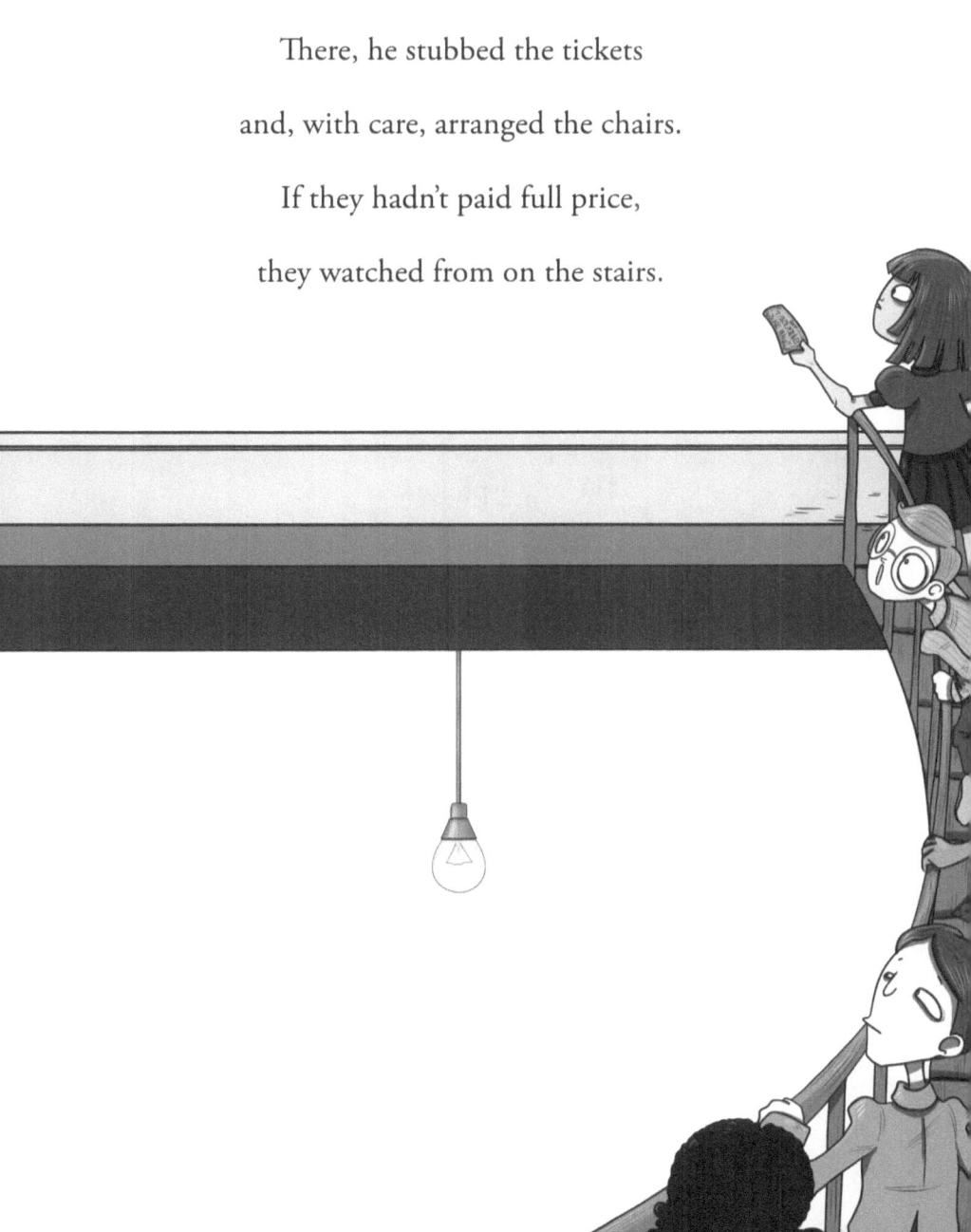

When every child was settled

Herbert's show, at last, commenced.

An eerie silence filled the room.

The atmosphere was tense.

With flair, he raised a bowl up high,

then dunked it in the sherbet.

The very last of all he'd got

heaped high in front of Herbert.

He stuck his head right in the dish.

He guzzled and he gorged.

Through all the sherbet mountains,

he gobbled and he forged.

This was no time for manners;

he crammed and stuffed the lot.

Resolute to eat each grain

till he was fit to pop.

Feeling sick, he soldiered on;

he reached the halfway mark.

His stomach grumbled noisily.

The sky outside went dark.

A wheezing and a gurgling

from his belly did abscond.

Several girls hid their eyes

in the fourth row and beyond.

Herbert, replete, endured his feast

and how his stomach grew.

One by one his buttons popped

and, round the room, they flew.

'Dearest friends, we near the end.

Don't let sorrow spoil the show.

For the life of me, I cannot think

of a tastier way to go.'

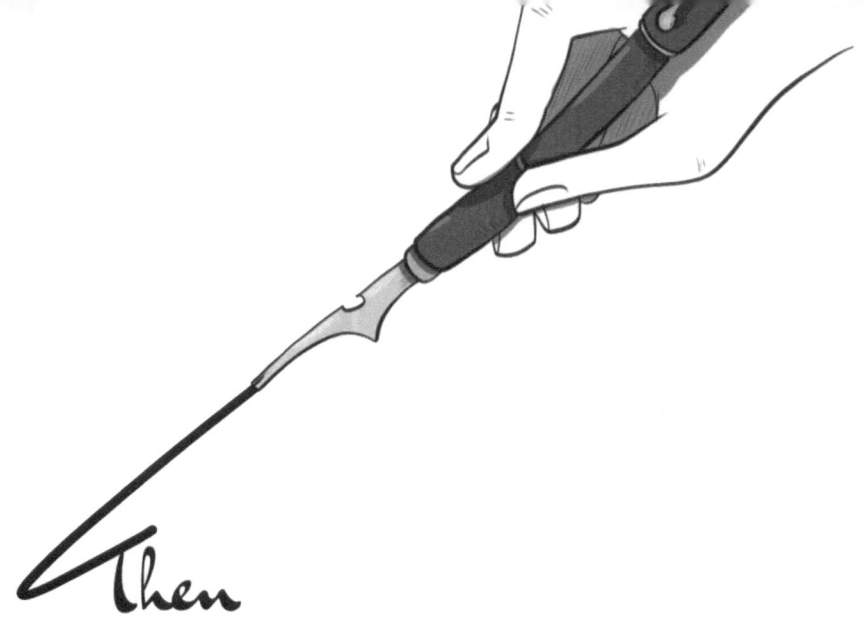

Then

he raised the final bowl,

pouring powder down his throat.

He grabbed a nearby Parker pen

and scrawled a farewell note.

All those gathered held their breath.

The crowd could take no more.

The boys they gasped, the girls they wept,

and panic filled row four.

Herbert burped

and Herbert belched,

then bulged like a balloon.

In fear, the children quickly fled

as Herbert filled the room.

Crowds mingled in the doorway.

Herbert gave a final wave.

The plucky few who risked a view

thought him very brave.

Rows of chairs were crushed below

as Herbert bloated more.

A budding artist seized his chance

and he began to draw.

Young Bert eclipsed the window

Darkness filled the room.

His classmates couldn't see a thing,

but they all heard the

BOOM!

When they dared look up again,

they saw a festive scene.

Sherbet fluttered down like snow

where Herbert once had been.

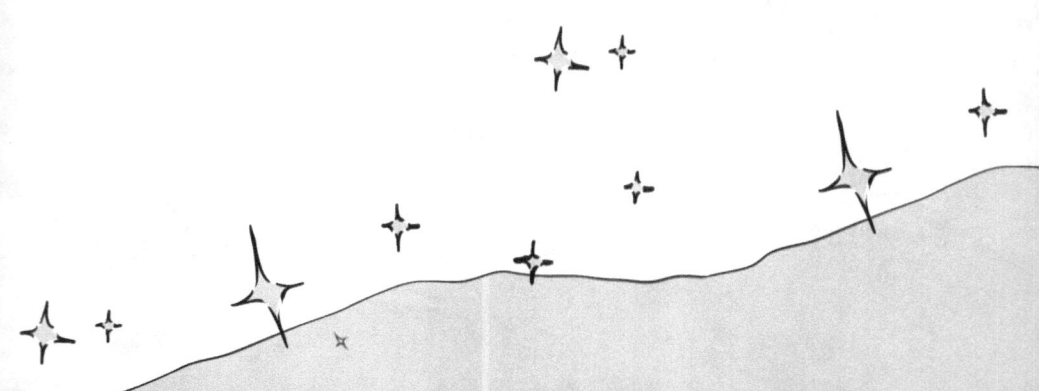

And when the flurry settled,

the children looked around.

All that was left of Herbert

was the sherbet on the ground.

An Ode to the Dearly Deceased

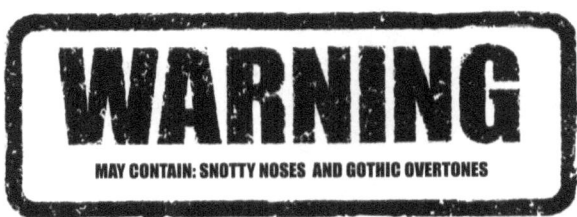

MAY CONTAIN: SNOTTY NOSES AND GOTHIC OVERTONES

The mourners were a-many,

their outfits rather bleak:

ebony hats and black cravats

created funeral chic.

Delivering doom

and dismal gloom,

they wound through narrow streets.

Lightning lit the troubled skies;

the rain came down in sheets.

It seemed to take forever,

that journey to the church:

beyond the post-box, by the school

and past a silver birch.

Amongst the damp, there hid a tramp;

just off the avenue.

Up he creaked, unsteadily,

to join their sombre crew.

Through the park, in the dusky-dark,

like ants they hurried on.

Over the heath, with chattering teeth

and vibes of woebegone.

Up the path: the sacred place.

They scurried on ahead.

Towards the tumbling turrets

and the dwelling of the dead.

Fog prowled around its mossy walls;

the air hung dank and chill.

The birds no longer twittered

at the church, all ghostly still.

The vicar,

pale and solemn,

stood waiting

in the porch.

Held within

his crooked hands,

a faintly glowing torch.

He bowed his head in deep respect.

The coffin bearers passed.

She had been a teeny thing,

the day she breathed her last.

And now inside, all bleary eyed,

they heard the tragic beat

of woeful music wafting

as they foraged for a seat.

The pews were packed with people;

bums filled extra chairs.

The vicar did a sermon

and ended with some prayers.

Then on into the graveyard,

they shuffled without sound

as gargoyles stared through stony eyes

down towards the ground.

The coffin looked so tiny;

the coffin looked so small

mused the creatures with foul features

hanging from the wall.

Below, the mourners gathered

to a dreary, eerie hush

till snivelling lanced the silence

and the tears began to gush.

Some blew their beaks in hankies.

Some wiped their snouts on sleeves.

One snotted on a nearby goat

(it's allowed when someone grieves).

Sob and shriek and sniffle.

Sadness filled the air.

The townsfolk wailed and whined and wept

and wallowed in despair.

They never would forget her.

In their minds, she'd never die.

Even though they'd said farewell.

Ciao. Cheerio. Goodbye.

The funeral finally over;

the family held a wake.

Serving out their sorrow

with cups of tea and cake.

The vicar was exhausted.

The coffin bearers spent.

The gravedigger had blistered hands;

his back was bowed and bent.

He sat beside the fire,

picking mud from crusty socks.

There'd been a lot of digging

for that tiny, nine-inch box.

The family, full of heartache,

found comfort in their cat

but they'd have swapped her any day

for their dear, departed rat.

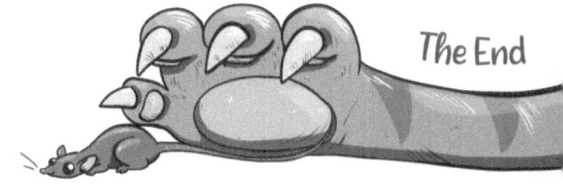

The End

Children

WARNING

THIS POEM IS FOR PARENTS ONLY

Babies are just highway-men;

robbers in disguise.

They strip you of your hard-earned cash

despite their tiny size.

And as they grow, they suck you dry

of everything you earn.

Cots and nappies, toys and games,

yet, what do they return?

Rattle designed by
Jimmy Chow

Dirt and poo and wee and puke

and farts and snot and dribble.

Perhaps you'll get a birthday card:

a splodge, a bodge, a scribble.

You clothe them and you feed them.

You let them live rent-free.

Then they ask for cash outright

the day that they turn three.

On it goes, as they grow:

currency and coin.

They'll borrow stuff they won't return –

they'll pocket, filch, purloin.

And when your handbag's empty

and your wallet's strapped for cash,

they'll gnaw away covertly

at your secret hidden stash.

$$\frac{d}{dx}\left[\frac{f(x)}{g(x)}\right] = \frac{g(x)f(x) - f(x)g(x)}{g(x)^2}$$

The strangest thing in all of this?

Most parents are quite smart.

Some of them have got degrees

in history, maths or art.

$+c$

$f(b) - f(a)$

$$\frac{d^2x}{dt^2} = -kx$$

$$\frac{df(x)}{dz}$$

$$\frac{dB}{dt} = -\frac{dC}{dt} = -\frac{dD}{dt} = (d_1)T^{\frac{1}{2}}AB - (d_2)T^{\frac{1}{2}}CD$$

$$F = mg = ma = m\frac{d^2h}{dt^2}$$

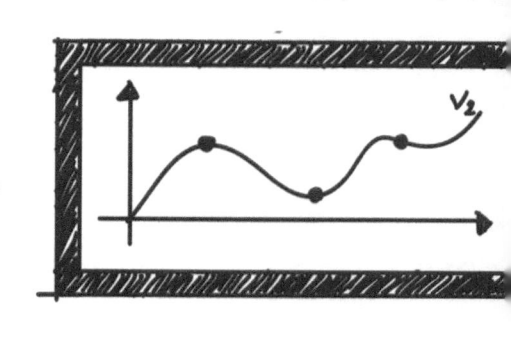

And yet their brains retire

when a baby comes along;

they never seem to realise

that the whole thing is a con.

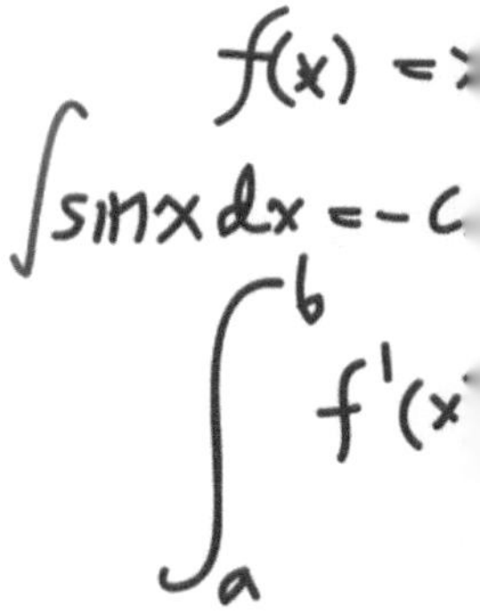

$$f(x) = x$$
$$\int \sin x \, dx = -c$$
$$\int_a^b f'(x$$

$$\left[x + \frac{b}{2a}\right]^2 = \frac{b^2 - 4ac}{4a^2}$$

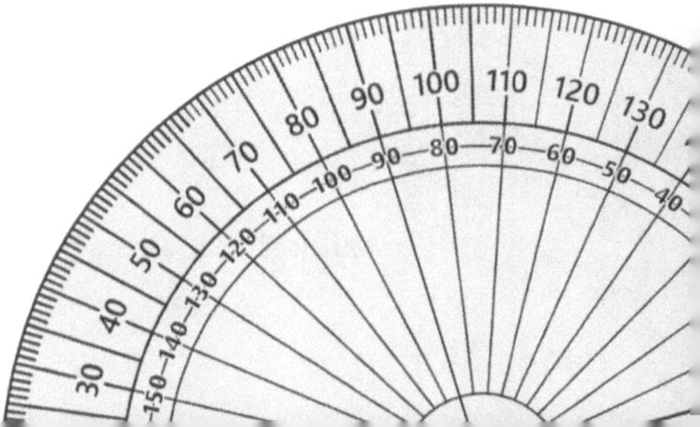

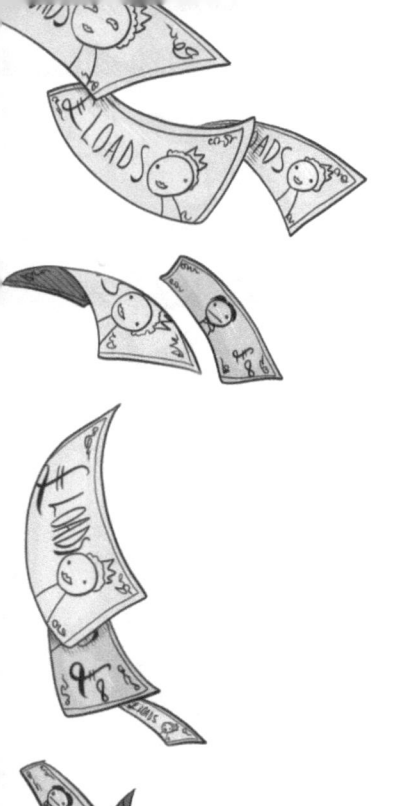

Christmas
Easter
Birthdays

Kids swindle and they scam.

(To think that it all started with an infant in a pram.)

And by the time the sprogs move out,

they've got you in their grasp.

They'll have you ping them money,

or send it out first class.

Now that they have flown the nest,

do you send a bill?

Or just grow old, sip at your tea

and put them in your will?

Here, you'll promise all the rest

(the bits they didn't take)

and they can sit and argue

who gets the biggest stake.

Has the penny finally dropped?

You've been taken for a ride.

And who is in the driving seat?

Darling Bonnie. Master Clyde.

The End

ABOUT THE AUTHOR

Marmalade Atkinson lives by the North Sea in a big, old house, full of candles. She writes in the dark early hours of the morning whilst the world sleeps.

Craven, her pet crow watches over her and pecks at the window as the sun rises. No one else in her family knows that Marmalade is a writer. It is something that she has kept secret for many years, but now, she would like to share her stories with you.

If you enjoyed this book let us know...
And tell all your friends about it too.
And your family ...
teacher ... the librarian ...
... the clown, the Devil and the old hag.

Get in touch: harry@markosia.com

The GIRL Who CRIED and CRIED
and further far-fetched fables

MARMALADE ATKINSON

with occasional meddling by New York Times bestselling author

G.P. TAYLOR

Want to read more? Why not check out the next book? The Girl WHo Cried and Cried is jam-packed with even more weird and wonderful children for you to read about. Meet Thomas, who likes to eat his own pets; Ethel, who won't stop crying; Bart, who bathes in a bin; and Dierdre, whose farts have made her famous!

www.ingramcontent.com/pod-product-compliance
Lightning Source LLC
Chambersburg PA
CBHW030342030726
47499CB00003B/878